MIRETTE
ON THE HIGH WIRE

Emily Arnold McCully

G.P. PUTNAM'S SONS · NEW YORK

G. P. Putnam's Sons, Reg. U.S. Pat. & Tm. Off. The scanning, uploading and distribution of this book via the Internet or via any other means without the permission of the publisher is illegal and punishable by law. Please purchase only authorized electronic editions, and do not participate in or encourage electronic piracy of copyrighted materials. Your support of the author's rights is appreciated. Published simultaneously in Canada.
Manufactured in China by South China Printing Co. Ltd. Book design by Nanette Stevenson. Lettering by David Gatti. The text is set in Goudy Old Style.
Library of Congress Cataloging-in-Publication Data: McCully, Emily Arnold. Mirette on the high wire / Emily Arnold McCully. p. cm. Summary: Mirette learns tightrope walking from Monsieur Bellini, a guest at her mother's boardinghouse, not knowing he is a celebrated tightrope artist who has withdrawn from performing because of fear. [1. Tightrope walking—Fiction.] I. Title. PZ7.M478415Mi 1992 91-36324 CIP AC [E]—dc20 ISBN 0-399-22130-1
17 19 20 18

One hundred years ago in Paris, when theaters and music halls drew traveling players from all over the world, the best place to stay was at the widow Gâteau's, a boardinghouse on English Street.

Acrobats, jugglers, actors, and mimes from as far away as Moscow and New York reclined on the widow's feather mattresses and devoured her kidney stews.

Madame Gâteau worked hard to make her guests comfortable, and so did her daughter, Mirette. The girl was an expert at washing linens, chopping leeks, paring potatoes, and mopping floors. She was a good listener too. Nothing pleased her more than to overhear the vagabond players tell of their adventures in this town and that along the road.

One evening a tall, sad-faced stranger arrived. He told Madame Gâteau he was Bellini, a retired high-wire walker.

"I am here for a rest," he said.

"I have just the room for you, Monsieur Bellini: in the back, where it's quiet," she said. "But it's on the ground floor, with no view."

"Perfect," said the stranger. "I will take my meals alone."

The next afternoon, when Mirette came for the sheets, there was the stranger, crossing the courtyard on air! Mirette was enchanted. Of all the things a person could do, this must be the most magical. Her feet tingled, as if they wanted to jump up on the wire beside Bellini.

Mirette worked up the courage to speak. "Excuse me, Monsieur Bellini, *I* want to learn to do that!" she cried.

Bellini sighed. "That would not be a good idea," he said. "Once you start, your feet are never happy again on the ground."

"Oh, please teach me!" Mirette begged. "My feet are already unhappy on the ground." But he shook his head.

Mirette watched him every day. He would slide his feet onto the wire, cast his eyes ahead, and cross without ever looking down, as if in a trance.

Finally she couldn't resist any longer. When Bellini was gone, she jumped up on the wire to try it herself. Her arms flailed like windmills. In a moment she was back on the ground. Bellini made it look so easy. Surely she could do it too if she kept trying.

In ten tries she balanced on one foot for a few seconds. In a day, she managed three steps without wavering. Finally, after a week of many, many falls, she walked the length of the wire. She couldn't wait to show Bellini.

He was silent for a long time. Then he said, "In the beginning everyone falls. Most give up. But you kept trying. Perhaps you have talent as well."

"Oh, thank you," said Mirette.

She got up two hours earlier every day to finish her chores before the sun shone in the courtyard. The rest of the day was for lessons and practice.

Bellini was a strict master. "Never let your eyes stray," he told her day after day. "Think only of the wire, and of crossing to the end."

When she could cross dozens of times without falling, he taught her the wire-walker's salute. Then she learned to run, to lie down, and to turn a somersault.

"I will never ever fall again!" Mirette shouted.

"Do not boast," Bellini said, so sharply that Mirette lost her balance and had to jump down.

One night an agent from Astley's Hippodrome in London rented a room.
He noticed Bellini on his way to dinner.

"What a shock to see him here!" he exclaimed.

"See who?" asked a mime.

"Why, the great Bellini! Didn't you know he was in the room at the back?"

"Bellini . . . the one who crossed Niagara Falls on a thousand-foot wire in ten minutes?" asked the mime.

"And on the way back stopped in the middle to cook an omelette on a stove full of live coals. Then he opened a bottle of champagne and toasted the crowd," the agent recalled.

"My uncle used to talk about that," said a juggler.

"Bellini crossed the Alps with baskets tied to his feet, fired a cannon over the bullring in Barcelona, walked a flaming wire wearing a blindfold in Naples—the man had the nerves of an iceberg," the agent said.

Mirette raced to Bellini's room.

"Is it true?" she cried. "You did all those things? Why didn't you tell me?
I want to do them too! I want to go with you!"

"I can't take you," said Bellini.

"But why not?" asked Mirette.

Bellini hesitated a long time. "Because I am afraid," he said at last.
Mirette was astonished. "*Afraid?*" she said. "But *why?*"
"Once you have fear on the wire, it never leaves," Bellini said.
"But you must *make* it leave!" Mirette insisted.
"I cannot," said Bellini.

Mirette turned and ran to the kitchen as tears sprang to her eyes. She had felt such joy on the wire. Now Bellini's fear was like a cloud casting its black shadow on all she had learned from him.

Bellini paced his room for hours. It was terrible to disappoint Mirette! By dawn he knew that if he didn't face his fear at last, he could not face Mirette. He knew what he must do. The question was, could he succeed?

That night, when the agent returned, Bellini was waiting for him. The agent listened to Bellini's plan with mounting excitement. "I'll take care of it," he promised. To himself he added, "A big crowd will make me a tidy profit. What luck I just happened to be in Paris now."

Bellini went out to find a length of hemp with a steel core. He borrowed a winch and worked until daylight securing the wire.

The next evening, Mirette heard the commotion in the street.

"Go and see what it is," her mother said. "Maybe it will cheer you up."

In the square was a hubbub. The crowd was so thick she couldn't see, at first, that the agent was aiming a spotlight at the sky.

". . . return of the great Bellini!" he was yelling. Could it be? Mirette's heart hammered in her chest.

Bellini stepped out onto the wire and saluted the crowd. He took a step and then froze. The crowd cheered wildly. But something was wrong. Mirette knew at once what it was. For a moment she was as frozen as Bellini was.

Then she threw herself at the door behind her, ran inside, up flight after
flight of stairs, and out through a skylight to the roof.

She stretched her hands to Bellini. He smiled and began to walk toward her. She stepped onto the wire, and with the most intense pleasure, as she had always imagined it might be, she started to cross the sky.

"Brava! Bravo!" roared the crowd.

"Protégée of the Great Bellini!" shouted the agent. He was beside himself, already planning the world tour of Bellini and Mirette.

As for the master and his pupil, they were thinking only of the wire, and of crossing to the end.